From Lullaby to Lullaby

By *Adèle Geras*

Illustrated by *Kathryn Brown*

Simon & Schuster Books for Young Readers

SIMON & SCHUSTER BOOKS FOR YOUNG READERS
An imprint of Simon & Schuster Children's Publishing Division
1230 Avenue of the Americas, New York, New York 10020
SIMON & SCHUSTER BOOKS FOR YOUNG READERS
is a trademark of Simon & Schuster.
Book design by Paul Zakris
The text of this book is set in 15-point symbol Medium
The illustrations are rendered in watercolor
Printed and bound in the United States of America
First Edition
10 9 8 7 6 5 4 3 2 1

LIBRARY OF CONGRESS CATALOGING-IN-PUBLICATION DATA

Geras, Adèle.
  From lullaby to lullaby / by Adèle Geras ;
illustrated by Kathryn Brown. — 1st ed.
    p. cm.
  Summary: A lullaby in which a parent, while knitting a
blanket for a child, describes the dreams of each of the
objects pictured in the blanket.
  ISBN 0-689-80568-3
  [1. Blankets—Fiction. 2. Dreams—Fiction. 3. Lullabies.
4. Stories in rhyme.]
  I. Brown, Kathryn, 1955–   ill. II. Title.
PZ8.3.G296Fr 1997 [E]—dc20 96-2958 CIP AC

For Sophie and Jenny—
good listeners to lullabies sung
by both their parents, years ago
—AG

For Sister, Mangrin, and Mattie,
Frankie's little friends
—KB

I took the silver singing needles
to make a blanket for your bed.
Rest your head,
close your eyes.
I'll knit you dreams and lullabies.

Here is a house.
Everyone's sleeping,
except a child
who wants to know
what everybody's dream might be;
and when they close their eyes at night,
what do they see?

Follow the yarns
as the yarns unwind.
What do you find?
What do you find?

Here is a doll
dreaming of walking
down the path to another house.
She dreams of a party,
and drinking tea
with all the friends
she has gone to see.

The narrow path that twists and bends
dreams of bringing you home
when your journey ends.

Follow the yarns.
What do you find?
What do you find
as the yarns unwind?

Here is a bear
who is brown and small
and wants to speak
in a small, brown voice,
so you can hear
the tales he tells
of big black bears
in caves of stone.
He whispers gently
in your ear:
"Look! Here I am.
You're not alone."

The dark cave dreams of sheltering
Mother and Father and Baby Bear,
keeping them dry, keeping them warm,
safe and cozy out of the storm.

What do you find
as the yarns unwind?
Follow the yarns.
What do you find?

Here is a rocking horse
standing still,
imagining fields
he can gallop through
when the moon is full
and the air is blue
and a green wind blows
from over the hill.

What the moon would love
is a mile of space
and no thin clouds to cover her face.

As the yarns unwind,
what do you find?
Follow the yarns.
What do you find?

Here is a kitten
with four white paws
on a rainbow day
in the meadow green.
She dreams of creeping
through the grass,
catching the butterflies
she has seen,
who tickle her white nose
as they pass.

Out in the meadow
a rainbow curves,
and as it fades
it longs to stay
fixed in its colors
for one whole day.

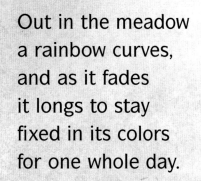

Follow the yarns.
What do you find?
As the yarns unwind,
what do you find?

Here is a ball,
rolling and rolling,
waiting to fly
from hand to hand,
waiting for beaches,
waiting for summer,
waiting for castles
made of sand.

The shell says: "Listen, listen to me.
Can you hear the sea, the sea, the sea?"

What do you find?
What do you find?
Follow the yarns
as the yarns unwind.

Here is a ship
with masts and spars
reaching up
to the silent stars.
This is a ship
that longs for an ocean
and longs to hear
the songs that are sung
under the water
in emerald caves
by the King of the Sea
and his mermaid daughter.

Up in the sky the small stars glow,
wanting the ship to follow their light
into the morning, out of the night.

Follow the yarns.
What do you find?
What do you find
as the yarns unwind?

Here is a train
that wants to run
clackety-clack
along the track,
all the way
to far away,
and all the way
back.

The mountain waits for a cloak of snow
when the winter comes and the blizzards blow.

Follow the yarns
as the yarns unwind.
What do you find?
What do you find?

Here is a tiger
dreaming of jungles
silent and shadowy,
full of prey.
He dreams of roaring,
snarling, clawing,
and an afternoon sleep
in the heat of the day.

A forest needs to be deep and wide
and dark to hide what it needs to hide.

What do you find
as the yarns unwind?
Follow the yarns.
What do you find?

Here is a rabbit
with pink glass eyes
who dreams of carrots
in long, straight rows.
He dreams of an open garden gate
and a place where frilly lettuce grows.

The garden waits for a summer day
and fuzzy bees to buzz and play.

As the yarns unwind,
what do you find?
Follow the yarns.
What do you find?

Here is a fish
in a bowl of glass,
dreaming of water flowing fast.
Dreaming of sliding and hiding away
by the riverbank,
in the reeds and grass.

As the river runs
it longs to reach
the wide gray sea,
the pebbly beach.

Follow the yarns.
What do you find?
As the yarns unwind,
what do you find?

Here is a bird
who wants to fly
out of the cage
with the golden bars,
out of the window,
into the sky,
where every tree
calls out and sings:
"Try it! Open them!
Spread your wings."

This is the wish
of every tree:
For birds to settle
among its leaves
and flutter and cry
and coo and call,
as summer slowly
turns to fall.

What do you find?
What do you find?
Follow the yarns
as the yarns unwind.

Here is a pillow
soft and white,
filled with every dream we know,
and also filled with songs that tell
where dreams come from,
where they go.

I wish the lamp could always be lit
so that I can sit in its light and knit . . .

a blanket to cover you
as you lie,
and as you move
from dream to dream,
from lullaby
to lullaby.

You followed the yarns
as the yarns unwound.
Rest your head.
Close your eyes.
Remember all the dreams you found.